THE MAYOR

Signs of Protest

MY COMMUNITY
THE MAYOR

Signs of Protest

by Patricia Lakin
pictures by Doug Cushman

RSVP
RAINTREE
STECK-VAUGHN
PUBLISHERS
The Steck-Vaughn Company

Austin, Texas

For Elizabeth Starkey, a tireless community activist.
And thanks to Robert Lawton, Jr.

A Lucas • Evans Book

Published by Raintree Steck-Vaughn Publishers,
an imprint of Steck-Vaughn Company

Library of Congress Cataloging-in-Publication Data
Lakin, Pat.
Signs of protest / by Patricia Lakin; pictures by Doug Cushman.
p. cm. — (My community)
"The mayor."
Summary: When the town has money problems, Edward, the mayor's nephew,
helps find a way for people to work together to meet the needs of
Parkside Elementary School and the Senior Citizen's Center.
ISBN 0-8114-8263-4
[1. City and town life—Fiction.   2. Politics, Practical—Fiction.]
I. Cushman, Doug, ill.   II. Title.   III. Series: Lakin, Pat.   My community.
PZ7.L1586Si   1995
[Fic]—dc20   94-19717
                                                           CIP
                                                           AC

Printed and bound in the United States
1 2 3 4 5 6 7 8 9 0 WZ 99 98 97 96 95 94

Right after school on Wednesday, Edward met Becka,
Tim, Jeff, and Rachel in front of the Springfield Town Hall.
They showed each other their protest signs.

Tim's sign said, HELP OUR TEACHERS.

Becka's read, DON'T BREAK PROMISES.

Edward had written HIRE AIDES on his.

5

"Will your uncle get mad at us?" Jeff asked Edward. "After all, we're against his plan. And he is the mayor here."

"I don't think so," said Edward. "He always says people should speak out when they think something is unfair."

6

Mrs. Yazzie, the principal at Parkside Elementary School, spoke to the gathering of parents, teachers, and students through a bullhorn. "We're going to march in a double line," she said.

"Everyone march in front of us," said Mr. Summers to the kids from his third-grade class. He walked beside Miss Yoo, the school nurse.

"And I'll make sure people and cars move along safely,"
Officer Tony Rollins told the protesters. He leaned on one of
the wooden horses that had been set up. Three other police
officers and two patrol cars were nearby.

Mr. Sullivan, the retired mail carrier, tapped Officer Rollins on the shoulder. "Where do I march?" he asked. He carried a sign in one hand and his cane in the other.

"I'm glad you want the town to hire teachers' aides, too," Rachel told Mr. Sullivan.

"But I don't!" he said. "If you get teachers' aides, there won't be enough money for our lunches at the senior citizens' center." His sign said, FEED US FIRST!

11

Edward heard Officer Rollins blow his whistle. He stopped
the cars so a group of senior citizens could cross the street.
They joined Mr. Sullivan. They looked mad and were carrying
signs, too.

12

"Are you protesting our protest?" asked Jeff.

"You got it, sonny," said Mr. Sullivan. "We're going to protest loud and clear at the town meeting. We were promised hot lunches. Now the mayor is saying he may have to take them away from us."

13

Now the senior citizens were shouting, "Feed us first!"

The students and teachers were saying, "S.O.S. Save Our School," over and over again.

"Some of the senior citizens don't have much money," said Rachel. "They need those lunches."

"I feel bad for both groups," said Edward. "But I feel bad for my uncle, too. As mayor, no matter what choice he makes, one group will be unhappy and angry."

Edward needed time to think. If only he could come up with a plan to help both groups.

After an hour, Mrs. Yazzie said that the town meeting was about to start.

The meeting room was filled with people. Edward's uncle sat up on the stage, next to the town treasurer. There was a big colored chart next to them, resting on an easel.

"Welcome," said Mayor Robert Schwartz after he banged the gavel. "I'm glad to see so many of you here, especially so many young people from Parkside Elementary School. I'd like to begin by asking if you youngsters have any questions."

Becka raised her hand. "Why can't the school hire teachers' aides like you promised?"

"Good question," said the mayor. Then he added, "Here are the facts. It all boils down to money and taxes."

Jeff raised his hand. "What do taxes have to do with it?"

"Everything," answered the mayor. "Tax money is used to run schools, build and repair roads, pay town workers, buy garbage trucks, and pay for other town services. But now the town won't get as much tax money as we thought it would."

Tim raised his hand. "Why wouldn't we get enough money? My folks say all they do is pay taxes!"

Lots of people in the audience smiled and agreed.

"Our problem started when our town's big factory closed down last spring," explained the mayor. He pointed to a chart on the easel. "We don't have the tax money from the factory anymore."

"My folks lost a lot of business in their hardware store when the factory closed," Becka whispered to Edward.

"My uncle worked at the factory. He lost his job," Tim told Edward. "He moved away to find another one."

"So," the mayor continued, "besides losing the taxes from the factory, we also lose taxes from people who moved away. Now our town has less money to spend. That's why we have to break some promises we made last spring."

"Like your promise for senior citizen lunches," someone shouted out.

"Please wait to be called on," said the mayor. "That way, everyone's opinion can be heard."

"Just like school," Edward whispered to Becka.

Suddenly Edward got an idea. Maybe they could solve their town's money problems the way they did in school. They had raised money with a bake sale or with a car wash. Edward got excited. After his uncle showed the audience more charts, Edward raised his hand.

"Yes?" the mayor called on Edward.

"Couldn't we raise money for the aides and senior citizen lunches through bake sales or car washes?"

"Good thinking, Edward," said the mayor. "But the cost of the aides and the lunches is very high. You'd have to hold bake sales and car washes every single day. That would take too much time away from your classwork."

Edward was disappointed that his idea wouldn't work.

"If only we could think of a partnership," said Becka.

"What do you mean?" Edward asked her.

"Remember when Mrs. Yazzie helped us start the school newspaper?" whispered Becka. "She got help from the town's newspaper."

Edward did remember. A partnership? He looked across the aisle at Mr. Sullivan. That was it. Mr. Sullivan could be part of the partnership.

Edward shot his hand up in the air.

"Yes, Edward?" his uncle said.

"We can solve the problem," he said in a loud, clear voice, "and everyone will be happy."

"How?" asked the town treasurer.

"Form a partnership. Why not ask the senior citizens to be the teachers' aides? They can eat lunch with us at school."

Mr. Sullivan scratched his head. "Well, I do like young
people, and I certainly have the time. But I'm not so sure
about this plan. How would I get to the school if the
sidewalks are icy and covered in snow?"

Rachel's mom raised her hand. "I'm the school's bus driver.
I would give up my lunch hour on days the weather is bad to
drive the seniors to and from Parkside."

Robert Schwartz stroked his chin. "This just might work," he said. He looked out at the audience. "How many senior citizens would be interested in helping out at the school? You could fill jobs like reading stories to some classes, filing, and photocopying."

Mr. Sullivan scratched his head again. Then his hand went up. Ten more senior citizens raised their hands, too.

"Come to think of it, I know some others who would like to help out," said Mr. Sullivan.

"Thanks to you, Edward, it looks like our town's problem may be solved," said Mayor Schwartz. "I'm proud of you."

Everyone turned to Edward and applauded.

"Want to be mayor?" his uncle shouted, after the applause had ended.

"Not yet," said Edward and laughed. "But maybe next year!"

Everyone laughed and applauded again.

31

Duties of a Mayor

- Discuss town's needs and problems at city council and community meetings

- Oversee all town offices such as:
  School board, Tax office, Health, Police, Recreation, Fire, and Sanitation Departments

- Review proposals offered by contractors

- Prepare town budget and review tax funds

- Make sure town follows local, state, and federal laws